LUCKY
SOCCER SAVE

BY JAKE MADDOX

text by
Colin Scharf

STONE ARCH BOOKS
a capstone imprint

Jake Maddox JV is published by Stone Arch Books, an imprint of Capstone.
1710 Roe Crest Drive
North Mankato, Minnesota 56003
www.capstonepub.com

Library of Congress Cataloging-in-Publication Data
Names: Maddox, Jake, author. | Scharf, Colin, author.
Title: Lucky soccer save / by Jake Maddox ; text by Colin Scharf.
Description: North Mankato, Minnesota : Stone Arch Books, a Capstone imprint, [2021] |
    Series: Jake Maddox JV | Audience: Ages 8–11. | Audience: Grades 4–6. | Summary:
    "Luis "Lucky" Martinez is the new kid on River Valley Junior High's JV soccer team.
    But his goalie skills aren't the only thing being tested. When a school talent show
    opens for auditions, Luis will find out if he's inherited his abuela's musical skills.
    Can Luis juggle both, or will he have to choose which of his passions to save: soccer
    or music?"— Provided by publisher.
Identifiers: LCCN 2020035142 (print) | LCCN 2020035143 (ebook) | ISBN 9781515882374
    (hardcover) | ISBN 9781515883456 (paperback) | ISBN 9781515892083 (pdf)
Subjects: CYAC: Soccer—Fiction. | Music—Fiction. | Puerto Ricans—Fiction.
Classification: LCC PZ7.M25643 Lu 2021 (print) | LCC PZ7.M25643 (ebook) |
    DDC [Fic]—dc23
LC record available at https://lccn.loc.gov/2020035142
LC ebook record available at https://lccn.loc.gov/2020035143

Designer: Dina Her

Image Credits
iStockphoto: technotr, Cover; Shutterstock: Brocreative, design element, Eky Studio, design
element, Gelner Tivadar, (ball) design element throughout, Isniper, design element

Printed and bound in the USA.   PO 3837

TABLE OF CONTENTS

CHAPTER 1

FEELING LUCKY

Luis Martinez sat in the bleachers at River Valley Park, listening to The Strikers in his headphones. He strummed an air guitar along with their punk rock soccer anthem, "Breakaway." It was his favorite song.

On the field, a dozen boys around his age played soccer. They launched passes through the air, blasted shots on goal, and played like they'd been teammates a long time.

Summer was almost over, and yet the world felt brand new. Luis and his papá had recently moved to

River Valley to help take care of his abuela. Abuela was really cool. She played piano and had been a singer when she was younger. Luis was excited to get to know her better.

Luis's cell phone vibrated with a text from Papá.

Dinner at 7. Arroz con gandules. Abuela's special recipe!

Yum! Luis typed back. *I'm at the park. See you at 7!*

Cheers rose up from the field as one of the goalies made a great save. Luis had been the goalie for his old team, at his old school. Luis liked playing goalie, but it also made him really nervous. The net was so big. Thinking about it sometimes made Luis feel anxious. The only thing that calmed him down was playing guitar.

On the field, a dark-haired striker dribbled toward the goal. He wound up for a shot, angling his foot like he would shoot to the right. The fake-out worked. The goalie dove right, and the shooter scored on the left side. His team cheered. The goalie dusted himself off, waved goodbye, and headed for the bike racks.

Luis's heart started pounding. *Maybe they'll ask me to play?*

One player waved in Luis's direction. Luis pulled off his headphones.

"Hey, new kid!" the boy shouted. He was tall and dark-skinned with curly black hair.

Luis looked around. "Me?"

The tall boy laughed. "Are there any other new kids up there?"

Luis's heart fluttered. He felt embarrassed. The other players had gathered around too. They all stared at him.

"Do you play?" the tall boy asked.

"Yeah," Luis replied. "I'm a goalie."

"Great!" The tall boy pointed to the empty net. "You're on my team."

Luis drew in a deep breath. *You can do this,* he told himself. The metal bleachers clanked beneath his sneakers as he hurried to the field.

The tall boy stuck out his hand. "I'm Kevin."

Luis slapped Kevin's hand for a low-five. "I'm Luis. People call me Lucky."

"Lucky Luis," Kevin said with a smile. The other boys laughed. "I hope you're feeling lucky today."

Luis hustled toward the goal. No matter how many times he approached a soccer net, the size of it always shocked him. How could one person ever keep a ball out of something so huge? Still, he had always managed to make the save. Last year, with his old team, Luis had a shutout season. Nobody scored on him. That was when he earned the nickname Lucky.

But this was a new town with new players. There was no telling how good he'd be until the shots started coming.

Luis positioned himself in the net and ran through his own special goalie ritual. He tapped each post, jumped to touch the crossbar, ran to the top of the goalie box, and jogged backward to the goal line. It helped him feel centered. He sang "Breakaway" in his head. The melody helped calm him too. He imagined the bleachers filled with cheering fans, just like the soccer stadiums at the games he watched on TV with Papá.

A kid with dyed green hair approached Luis. He wore a Strikers band T-shirt. *Whoa!* Luis thought. *Maybe he's a musician too!*

"I'm Joe," said the green-haired boy. "I play defense. The only guy you have to worry about is Scott." Joe pointed to the dark-haired striker who had scored on the previous goalie. "He likes to fake right and shoot left."

"Thanks." Luis was about to say something about Joe's Strikers T-shirt, but then Kevin shouted from midfield.

"Ready, Lucky?"

Luis gave a thumbs-up.

Kevin kicked the ball to a midfielder, and Luis's team pushed up the field. Kevin deked around a defender and dribbled toward the net. The goalie rushed out to tackle the ball away, but Kevin was too fast. He darted around the keeper and booted the ball into the net.

Goal!

The team cheered and high-fived Kevin. Luis cheered from the goal.

Soon the ball was back in play and hurtling down the field. Scott, the dark-haired striker, dribbled around Luis's teammates. Scott was really fast, and he was getting closer to Luis. Scott's teammates called for passes, but Scott kept the ball for himself. He threw a shoulder into Joe, sending him crashing to the grass.

"That was a foul, Scott!" Joe shouted.

Scott didn't stop. Now, Luis was the only person between Scott and the goal.

Luis took a deep breath, and everything seemed to slow down. Scott's feet danced around the ball as if in slow motion. Luis could see the bits of mud and grass staining the ball's black-and-white pattern. It was nothing more than leather and rubber and air. All Luis had to do was get between it and the net. Simple.

Then, just like Joe had said, Scott faked to the right, then blasted a shot high and to the left. Luis leapt through the air and blocked the ball with his outstretched hands. He fell to the grass with a *thud*.

The ball lay a foot away. Another striker dashed in for the rebound, but Luis scrambled to cover the ball. The attacking team backed off. Luis's teammates rushed up cheering.

"That was amazing!"

"Great save!"

Kevin high-fived Luis. "That's why they call you Lucky!"

Luis grinned. It felt as if a huge weight had just been lifted from his shoulders. In a matter of seconds, that save had turned him from new kid to hero.

They played a little while longer. Luis made a few more saves, but none were as impressive as that first one. Soon, they called it quits. Luis's team won 5–2. Everyone headed for the bike racks to pedal home. Kevin and Joe caught up with Luis.

"Tryouts for JV soccer are coming up," Kevin said. "You should come, Lucky. We could use a great goalie like you."

"Oh, um . . . ," Luis started. He felt excited to play with the guys on a real team. But the thought of trying out for JV made his stomach tighten. Last year, as a seventh-grader, Luis had played on the modified team. Mostly ninth- and tenth-graders played JV. If Luis made the team, he'd be facing players much older and bigger than him.

"Trust me, Lucky," Kevin said. "You're the best goalie I've ever seen."

Well, if Kevin thinks so . . . , Luis thought.

"Sure," he said out loud. "I'll be there."

"Awesome!" Kevin said, then biked away.

Luis stood with Joe. "What were you listening to up in the bleachers?" Joe asked. "It looked like you were playing air guitar."

Luis pointed at Joe's shirt. "The Strikers."

Joe's eyes widened. "You know The Strikers?"

"They're my favorite band," Luis replied. "I can play most of their songs on guitar—real guitar, not just air."

"A great goalie with great taste in music, *and* you're a guitarist!" Joe said. "Where did you come from?"

Luis shrugged. "We just moved here."

"I play drums," Joe said. "We should start a band!"

Luis's heart started pounding. The idea of starting a band with Joe made him even more excited than trying out for the JV team.

"That'd be awesome!" Luis said. He was still the new kid, but he was starting to feel like he belonged.

CHAPTER 2

PRACTICE MAKES PERFECT

Abuela lived in a brick house on a tree-lined street on the north side of River Valley. Her house smelled of roses, coffee, and fried tortillas. Little Puerto Rican flags poked up out of flowerpots on top of the old upright piano in the den. Luis liked to sit at the piano, picking out the tunes from his favorite songs.

Right now, he was working on "Breakaway." Luis danced his fingers around the keys. He could already play the chords on his guitar, but there was something magical about the sound of Abuela's old piano.

Papá came into the room. He wore a red and yellow soccer jersey. "Lucky, dinner's ready."

The delicious smell of onions, peppers, and cilantro wafted in from the kitchen. But Luis kept playing piano. He wasn't hungry for food. He was hungry for music. He was really excited about starting a band with Joe, but he felt nervous about telling Papá. Papá wanted Luis to become a great soccer player, not a musician.

"Vamos, hijo," Papá said. "You can play music later. Abuela is hungry."

"Okay," Luis replied. He pulled himself away from the piano keys. "I'm coming."

Abuela sat at the dining room table. Her curly white hair matched the white frames of her big glasses. She wore gold bracelets and a fuzzy purple robe. "Hola, nieto," she said as Luis walked in. "I heard you playing piano. You're musical just like your abuela."

Even when she wasn't singing, Abuela's voice sounded like a song. She reached out for a hug, and

Luis went to her. She hugged him and kissed his cheeks. "Someday, you'll be a big music star."

"Gracias, Abuela," Luis replied with a smile. He sat down between his abuela and papá. Soon they were digging into their plates of arroz con gandules. The dish was a traditional Puerto Rican meal of rice, peas, and spices. Abuela made it the best. The scent alone made Luis's mouth water.

"You know, musicians get into a lot of trouble, Lucky," Papá said between bites. "But soccer keeps you strong and healthy. Besides, you're a great goalie. Remember your shutout season last year? You've got a real talent!"

"He's got a real talent for music too," Abuela said. "And music keeps a person strong and healthy in ways that sports can't."

"Sure, Mamá," Papá said. He turned to Luis. "Did you make any friends at the park today?"

Luis nodded. "A bunch of kids were playing soccer. One goalie left. They asked me to play."

Papá perked up. "That's great! Did you show them why you're called Lucky?"

Luis nodded and told Papá about the save on Scott. Describing the moment brought on a rush of excitement through him.

"I wish I could've seen you!" Papá said. "You're going to try out for the JV team, right?"

Luis shrugged. "Some of the guys said I'm the best goalie they've ever seen," he said. "I also met a kid named Joe. He has green hair, and he was wearing a Strikers T-shirt, and he's a—"

"I'll *bet* you're the best goalie they've ever seen, Lucky!" Papá interrupted. "You're the best goalie *I've* ever seen! And I've been playing soccer my whole life!"

Luis shrugged again and asked, "Can I be excused?" He wanted to go play his guitar.

"Finish your dinner," Papá said, "and then let's kick the ball around while there's still daylight. We have to get you ready for tryouts!"

Luis frowned. "But Papá, I already spent most of the day playing soccer. I want—"

Abuela interrupted to ask about Joe. "Your new friend has green hair?"

"Yeah," Luis said. "Joe has really cool green hair, and he was wearing a Strikers T-shirt. They're my favorite band. They have a song about soccer. Joe is also a drummer, and we're going to start a band—"

"Green-haired kids?" Papá said. "Sounds like a good way to get into trouble."

"A band!" Abuela said. "How fun! I was your age when I started performing, you know."

"Really?" Luis was excited to learn about Abuela's musical past. "What was it like? Were you nervous?"

Abuela smiled. "Oh, it was so long ago I hardly remember." She motioned to Papá, who had finished his dinner and was rinsing dishes in the sink. "Go play with him. I'll tell you music stories another time."

Luis smiled too. "Gracias, Abuela." He couldn't wait to hear more.

The setting sun cast a golden glow over Abuela's backyard. Luis watched Papá juggle a soccer ball from knee to knee. Papá had played soccer every day as a kid growing up in Puerto Rico, and he was still a great player. Luis's earliest memories were of chasing a soccer ball around with Papá.

Now Papá dropped the ball and dribbled toward Luis. "Try to steal it from me," he said.

Luis stuck out his foot to poke the ball away, but Papá did his famous rainbow kick, launching the ball high over their heads. He darted around Luis, trapped the ball, and booted it between the two pine trees they used for a goal.

"Martinez scores!" Papá cheered.

Luis collected the ball from the pines and dribbled toward Papá. As a goalie, he didn't have much use for tricks like rainbow kicks, or even dribbling, since he was able to use his hands. Still, Papá always said that the best players were well-rounded. Strikers, midfielders, defenders, and goalies should be able to trade positions. So, over the years, Luis had gotten pretty good at every position. But he liked playing goalie best.

Papá ran up to steal the ball. Luis tried to deke around him. Papá was too fast. He knocked the ball through Luis's legs and fired it through the pine trees.

"*Goooaaal!*" Papá shouted like a TV announcer. "The crowd goes wild!"

Luis grabbed the ball and started walking across the lawn back to Abuela's house.

"Hey, que pasó?" Papá ran up to Luis. "I thought we were having fun."

Luis kept walking. "I played enough soccer today. I just want to play my guitar."

"We can slow it down," Papá said. "You're doing everything right. I've just been playing longer. If we get you good enough to beat me, you'll be able to beat anybody!"

"But I'm a goalie, Papá. I don't need to know how to do that stuff."

Papá put a hand on Luis's shoulder. "Remember what I said about well-rounded players? They become the best. As a goalie, you need to know how strikers think so you can stop them."

Luis nodded. "I remember."

Long shadows from the pine trees spilled across the grass. The sun had all but disappeared. Papá rushed into the house and came back with a speaker, and soon the opening chant of "Breakaway" filled the yard.

The music hit Luis's ears like a breath of fresh air. He remembered how Abuela said that he would become a great musician someday. The music and Abuela's words filled him with new energy. Luis played with Papá until the full moon glowed like a big soccer ball in the night sky.

CHAPTER 3

TRYOUTS

The air at River Valley Park smelled of fresh-cut grass. Luis kicked a ball with Kevin and Joe, waiting for tryouts to start. The scent of grass and the sounds of feet kicking soccer balls reminded Luis of his old friends and teammates. He missed them.

The coach blew a whistle. "Let's get started, boys!" he yelled. Everybody huddled together.

Luis stood beside Kevin and Joe. "Coach Anderson is going to love your goalie moves, Lucky," Kevin said, keeping his voice low while the coach spoke.

23

"Yeah? Cool," Luis said.

"You'll make starter for sure—"

Another whistle surprised them both. "Kevin!" Coach Anderson shouted. "When I'm talking, you're listening."

"Sorry, Coach," Kevin said.

Coach Anderson narrowed his eyes at Luis. "What's your name?"

"Luis Martinez."

"Luis is new," Joe said. "He's a great goalie. His nickname is Lucky."

Coach Anderson smiled. "Well, we've already got a lucky goalie in Tony. Luis will have to prove he's luckier."

A tall boy with red hair turned around and sized up Luis. He sneered as if to say, *Good luck taking my position.*

After Coach had finished his talk, the boys lined up for stretches. Luis was by far the most flexible. He could place both palms flat on the grass and nearly

24

slip into a full split. His flexibility had helped him make big saves for his old team.

Coach Anderson seemed impressed too. "Lucky?" he said. "Your nickname should be Bendy."

The other boys laughed. Luis felt embarrassed, even though being flexible wasn't a bad thing. He kept his head down and deepened his stretch. He felt that good burn throughout his legs.

Then the boys ran laps. Kevin led the pack. He was the fastest, followed by Scott. Luis kept pace in the middle of the group. He ran beside two boys he remembered from the park. Their names were Wayne and Brendan.

"You made some awesome saves the other day," said Wayne.

"You'll be our starter for sure," said Brendan.

Excitement rushed through Luis's body, like when he listened to his favorite music. He had been the starting goalie on his last team. That meant he had started every game off in the goal, rather than on the bench. Starters got to play more. The thought pushed Luis to run even faster, and he finished near the front of the team.

Next, Coach Anderson made everyone partner up for dribbling and passing drills. Kevin waved at Lucky. "Let's be partners."

Kevin kicked a high pass that Luis trapped with his chest. Then Luis popped the ball up onto his knee and juggled it back and forth, just like Papá. Luis noticed Coach Anderson looking in his direction. He was definitely watching.

"You've got moves, Lucky," Kevin said. "But let's see if you can stop this one!"

Kevin tried to deke past Luis. His move was similar to one of Papá's. Luis stole the ball away with ease.

"Whoa!" Kevin said. "You're the first person to stop my move!"

Luis smiled. "My dad pulls that one on me all the time."

A whistle sounded for the boys to gather in for shooting drills. Coach Anderson sent Tony to the goal, then pointed at Luis. "You're up next," he said.

The boys took turns shooting on Tony. His reflexes were great. He stopped every shot, even Kevin's. No wonder he was the starter.

Luis studied the shooters. He watched how they positioned their bodies, how their heads moved, and which side of the net they aimed for. Papá had taught him to watch for tells—the little movements that were clues to how a player would shoot. He was starting to feel nervous. His stomach knotted up and his breath came quick.

Joe walked up beside him. "Hey, I'm excited to start our band, Lucky. We can jam in my garage. I have an amp. You just need to bring your guitar. Want to come over on Saturday?"

Luis looked at Joe's green hair. He worried what Papá would say. But he really wanted to start a band.

"Yeah, sure," Luis said. "That'd be awesome."

Joe grinned and gave him a fist bump. "Great!"

Luis bounced in place to the rhythm of the music in his head. He felt much less nervous after talking with Joe. What would they call their band? Who would sing? Who would play bass? For a little while, Luis forgot all about soccer.

The butterflies started buzzing again in Luis's stomach, though, when Scott stepped up to shoot on Tony. Scott stepped back from the ball and shifted his weight from his right leg to his left. Then he rushed up and swung his leg like he would blast a shot to the right.

It was a trick, and Tony fell for it. He dove to the right, leaving the left side of the net wide open. Scott slammed the ball into the goal.

It was the same move he pulled at the park! Luis thought. That was Scott's move—he liked to fake right, then shoot left.

Coach blew the whistle. "All right. You're in, Martinez!"

Luis drew a deep breath and jogged toward the goal. He quickly ran through his ritual, and then the shots came flying in. Luis made saves easily. He scooped up low rolling shots. He jumped for high shots. He even used his head to redirect the ball over the crossbar.

When Scott lined up to shoot, a lull fell over the field. Birds chirped in the trees. Somewhere, a car horn honked. Scott's cleats brushed over the grass.

Luis watched. He was ready. He heard "Breakaway" start to play in his mind.

Scott dribbled forward. Luis watched his feet, waiting for Scott to try the fake.

Which is exactly what he did.

Just like before, Scott shifted his weight. It was a tiny move—his tell—but Luis noticed it. Then Scott faked to the right and slammed the ball hard to the left.

Luis knew what to do. He leapt through the air as if pulled by a wire. He caught the ball and pulled it tight to his body as he landed. No rebound this time.

Coach Anderson blew the whistle. "Great save, Martinez!" he said. "I see why they call you Lucky."

Scott and Tony glared at Luis, but he ignored them. Once again, he'd impressed everybody with his save. He felt proud of himself. He saw Joe cheering on the sideline, and the thrill of starting a band rushed through him too. Luis was starting to feel pretty lucky.

CHAPTER 4

BAND PRACTICE

That Saturday, Luis told Papá he was meeting
friends to play soccer at the park. Instead, he biked to
Joe's with his guitar gig bag strapped to his back. He
didn't like lying. But he was afraid that Papá would
tell him he couldn't play music, that Luis should focus
on soccer instead. This was the only way he could
follow his music dreams.

When he arrived at Joe's house, Luis saw his
green-haired friend and a girl he didn't know in
the garage. The girl was tuning up a bass.

"What's up, Lucky?" Joe asked. "This is Sheena. She's our bassist!"

"Hey, Lucky," Sheena said, giving him a wave. She seemed cool. She wore white low-top sneakers, ripped blue jeans, and a sweater with a cat flying over a mountain range. Beaded bracelets jingled on her wrists. Thin gold-hoop earrings peeked out from her brown hair. But most impressive was her shiny, white bass guitar.

"Rad bass," Luis said.

"Thanks." Sheena pointed to his guitar case. "What's in there?"

Luis unzipped the bag. He pulled out his electric guitar. The paint was sparkly gold. It was a vintage model, and Luis thought that made it even cooler.

The guitar had belonged to Papá when he was Luis's age. Luis had been begging Papá for a guitar, so he had given it to Luis as a birthday present. Papá never really learned to play. He had told Luis he just didn't have "it" when it came to music. For the past two years, Luis had been teaching himself guitar from watching online videos. Sometimes he would practice quietly for hours after Papá was asleep.

"Wow," Sheena said. "That guitar is beautiful!"

"We're going to have the coolest band!" Joe shouted from behind his drum set. His shiny cymbals looked like big gold plates on their stands.

Joe started playing a simple beat. Sheena joined in. Her bass shook the entire garage. Her fingers moved quickly. She was a great player.

Luis rushed to plug his guitar into Joe's amp. They jammed for half an hour without a single word. They were learning how the others played. The music spoke for them.

Finally, Joe brought the jam to a close with a big cymbal crash. "Do you want to try to learn a song?" he asked.

"Sure!" Luis said. He started to show Sheena the chords for The Strikers' "Breakaway," but she cut him off.

"I love The Strikers!" she said. "I can play their whole album."

"Then let's rock!" Joe said. He clicked his drumsticks. "One, two, three, four—"

Joe started pounding the drums. Luis and Sheena filled the garage with sound. Until that moment, Luis had only ever played along with the song on his stereo. It felt amazing to play with a real drummer and real bassist. Luis jumped around and sang the lyrics at the top of his lungs. Joe and Sheena joined him on the chorus.

When they reached the end of the song, Luis stepped onto the kick drum like he'd seen Paul Striker do in The Strikers' music videos. Then he jumped off and strummed the last chord in time with Joe's final crash. Sheena jumped high too. She did a cool kick in midair.

"That was awesome!" Joe said. "We have to talk to Ms. Mellor about playing in the fall talent show!"

"Who's Ms. Mellor?" Luis asked between heavy breaths. He felt as if he had just played a full soccer match.

"The music teacher," Sheena said. "She's going to love us!"

School started next week. Luis had been curious about the music classes at River Valley Junior High. His old school was small and didn't have much of a music program. Kids there were mostly interested in sports, which had been okay because Luis was a good soccer player. Still, he wished the music classes had been stronger.

"What's the talent show like?" Luis asked.

"First, you audition. If you're good enough, you get to play," Sheena said. "It's a lot of karaoke. The jazz band and show choir perform. But nobody has ever had a rock band. If we get in, we'll bring the house down."

A wave of nerves hit Luis. What would Papá think about all of this?

"We'll need a band name," Joe said.

"And a singer," Sheena added.

Joe pointed a drumstick at Luis. "I heard you belting it out. You've got my vote!"

"Yeah!" Sheena nodded. "You sounded great!"

Luis blushed. Abuela was the only person who had ever said he was a good singer, but a burst of excitement rushed through him. "You sure?"

"Don't sweat it. You're a natural," Sheena replied. "Plus I'll back you up by singing harmonies."

"Let's play it again!" Joe said.

Joe started the drumbeat. Luis sang with even more attitude. When they finished the song, they were all sweaty, red-faced, and smiling.

"Do you guys know anything by Love Badgers?" Sheena asked. She started playing one of their songs called "Keep On Walking." It was really catchy, and Sheena had a great voice. Luis watched her fingers for the notes, then joined in on guitar. Joe drummed, and they rocked through the song.

Luis closed his eyes and saw himself on a stage. White spotlights beamed down. A crowd of people danced and sang along as he and Joe and Sheena rocked through the night. He felt alive.

CHAPTER 5

THE GOALIE ZONE

River Valley Junior High was really different from Luis's old school. It was huge. There were at least three hundred students in each grade. Luis could roam the halls and almost never see the same person twice. This made it easier to be the new kid.

Luckily, Luis had made the JV team and had made friends with guys from soccer. After two weeks of school, he now felt more at home. Their first game was in a few days, but Coach Anderson still hadn't announced the starting goalie. Papá, Kevin, and Joe all thought Luis would become the starter. But Luis had his doubts.

Luis had two classes with Kevin and Sheena, and only one with Joe—Music Appreciation with Ms. Mellor. Luis really liked the class. They had spent the first few days talking about their favorite music. When Luis said his favorite band was The Strikers, Ms. Mellor said she liked them too. None of Luis's other teachers knew any of the music he liked.

Now, on their way to Music Appreciation, Joe was finally going to ask Ms. Mellor about auditioning for the talent show. The band had been playing together every day after soccer practice. Luis had told Papá that soccer went later than it did. He didn't know why he felt scared to tell Papá the truth, but for now he was keeping it to himself.

"Are you sure we're ready to audition?" Luis asked Joe. Even with all that practice, Luis felt uneasy. "I'm still having trouble singing and playing some of the parts."

Joe laughed. "You worry too much, Lucky! Just pretend you're in the goal and you've got that Goalie Zone thing happening."

"Goalie Zone thing?" Luis repeated.

"Yeah, like when you get real calm," Joe explained. "You're in the zone."

Luis had never really thought of it that way. "Maybe we should see how this weekend's rehearsal goes," he said, "then ask Ms. Mellor."

A woman spoke up from behind them. "What did you want to ask me?"

The boys turned. Ms. Mellor wore a white sweater, black skirt, and leopard-print shoes. Gold bracelets clinked on her wrists. She looked like she might be the singer in a band.

Luis blushed. "Uh," he said. "Hi, Ms. Mellor."

"We were going to ask—" Joe started.

"Nothing!" Luis piped up. "We weren't going to ask anything!"

Ms. Mellor smirked. "Nothing, eh? Well, if nothing turns into something, let me know. Now, take your seats. Class is starting."

Luis felt like a fool as he and Joe shuffled into the classroom.

Ms. Mellor broke the class into four singing sections—sopranos, altos, tenors, and baritones. The girls sang soprano and alto. Many of the boys sang in low, quiet voices. Luis had a higher voice and found himself singing with the tenors. Some of the boys snickered. Luis tuned them out and focused on the music.

In the back of his mind, Luis thought about what Joe had said. As soon as Luis stepped in front of the goal, his mind always sharpened into focus—no matter how nervous he was. Maybe Joe was right. Luis just needed to turn Goalie Zone into Guitar Zone.

When the bell rang, Ms. Mellor called Luis and Joe to her desk. "So, boys," she began. "Did nothing turn into something?"

"Well . . . ," Luis stalled.

Joe took over. "We started a band. We're really good. Lucky sings and plays guitar, I play drums, Sheena plays bass, and we want to audition for the talent show!"

"Oh." Ms. Mellor smiled. "Is that all?"

Luis shrugged. "Yeah."

"Certainly," Ms. Mellor said. "How about next Wednesday after school?"

"Sounds great!" Luis said. They would get the weekend to rehearse after all!

Ms. Mellor got out the sign-up sheet. "So, what's your band called?"

Luis said, "We don't have a name yet—"

"We're Lucky Save!" Joe blurted. He winked at Luis.

Luis gave him a confused look. *Lucky Save? Where did that come from?*

"Lucky Save, huh?" Ms. Mellor smirked. "Sounds like a band that sings about soccer."

"We do have a song about soccer," Joe said. "It's super cool. It's called 'Breakaway' and it's by The Strikers. We'll play that at our audition!"

Ms. Mellor told them they'd better practice hard. "Lots of students are already signed up," she said, "and we only have so many performance slots."

"Don't sweat it, Ms. M," Joe said. "We'll knock your socks off!"

Ms. Mellor laughed. "I'll bring an extra pair."

Luis and Joe ran down the hall, excited for Lucky Save to rock the school.

CHAPTER 6

THE GUITAR LISTENS

Luis strummed his guitar in his bedroom, practicing singing and playing at the same time. It was a balancing act, almost like juggling a soccer ball and trying to make saves at the same time. But when he closed his eyes and got himself in the zone, he could sing and play just fine. Now he understood what Joe had meant.

"Hola, Luisito," Abuela said. She stood in the doorway. "Can I come in?"

The scent of Abuela's perfume filled the room and made Luis think of pink flowers. She sat on the bed beside him. "When I was your age," she said, "I learned to play as many instruments as possible."

"Really?" Luis asked.

Abuela nodded. "I loved music so much. Mamá was a great piano player, and she could sing like an angel. Mi papá too. He could play guitar, trumpet, accordion. I see a lot of him in you. You're always singing to yourself, and that guitar is practically attached to you."

Luis looked at his guitar. Abuela was right. He never wanted to put it down. He loved the feel of the strings beneath his fingers, the different chord shapes, and the feeling of possibility. He could channel all his feelings into his guitar. The guitar listened. It encouraged him. It relaxed him. Playing guitar made him feel like he could do anything.

"I bought that guitar for your father," Abuela said. "Did you know that?"

Luis nodded. "Papá told me that."

"He has a little bit of music in him, too, but he fell in love with soccer. Ever since he was your age, that's all he wanted to do."

"Papá loves soccer more than anything," Luis said.

"Your papá is very passionate, just like you," Abuela said. Then she tapped the guitar. "Por favor, Luisito? Can I play?"

Luis was excited. "You play guitar?"

"Oh," Abuela said, pinching together her thumb and forefinger and peering at Luis through the narrow gap. "Un poquito."

"Cool!" Luis handed over the guitar.

"Rock and roll!" Abuela joked. Luis switched off the amp and watched Abuela settle her thin fingers on the strings. She shaped a G chord, a D, then a C, humming a little tune to herself. Luis watched her right hand, waiting for her to strum.

"Dios mío," Abuela said, pulling her fingers off. "These steel strings hurt my poor old fingers!"

"What were you trying to play?" Luis asked.

"Oh, just some old song I used to know."

"Can you play it? Please?"

Just then, Papá stepped into the room. He wore his soccer jersey, soccer shorts, and cleats. "Lucky! Any word if you're going to start in goal on Saturday?"

Luis shook his head. "Coach hasn't announced the starters yet."

"Well, let's go work on your penalty kicks," Papá said. "Those saves will make or break a game."

"But . . ." Luis motioned to Abuela. "Abuela's going to play me a song."

Papá sighed. "Okay. I'll be outside if you want to come play."

Abuela handed the guitar back to Luis. "It's okay. Go. I'll play you a song some other time."

"No, Abuela, I want to—"

"Run along," Abuela said. "Sounds like you've got a big chance with your team. You want to be sure you're ready!"

Luis put his guitar back into its case and followed Papá out to the backyard. They settled into the rhythm of goalie practice. But Luis was worried about Lucky Save being good enough for the audition. He kept giving up goals.

"Get your head in the game, Luis!" Papá shouted, after scoring five goals in a row. "You'll never make starter playing like this!"

"Sorry," Luis said. He closed his eyes and took a long, deep breath. He sang "Breakaway" to himself, trying to get back into his Goalie Zone. He saw a stadium filled with cheering fans. He saw the opposing strikers closing in on goal. Every muscle in his body locked in with the movements of that imaginary soccer ball.

"Ready, hijo?" Papá said.

Luis opened his eyes. "I'm ready."

Papá smiled. "Okay." He dribbled the ball around the yard. Birds chirped in the trees. Traffic whooshed along the main road. Papá's cleats swished through the grass. Luis felt an invisible thread connecting him to the soccer ball. He'd found his zone.

Now Papá moved his shoulders in a way to shake Luis's concentration. This was Papá's tell. Luis knew this meant he was going to shoot, and the ball would go to the right.

Thwack! Papá kicked the ball, sending it high and to the right. Luis exploded off the ground and caught the ball.

"That's it, hijo!" Papá shouted. "That's why they call you Lucky!"

They played until sunset. At one point, Luis heard music drifting along a breeze. It sounded like Abuela singing softly in Spanish.

CHAPTER 7

THE STARTING GOALIE IS...

The next day, Coach Anderson blew the whistle at the end of practice. "Take a knee, boys," he said. "I'm going to announce the starting lineup."

Luis's heart raced. Practice had been easy, with light passing and shooting drills, followed by a scrimmage. During the scrimmage, Luis and Tony had each allowed one goal, and the match ended in a tie.

Luis felt like he had made more difficult saves, though, including one where he had spilled the rebound and needed to scramble to cover the ball from Scott's swinging feet. The only goal Luis had allowed came off a corner kick that somebody head-butted past him. There wasn't much he could've done about that one.

On the other end of the field, Tony had let a blast from Kevin sail over his head. Other than that, though, Tony's defensemen had kept the shots to a minimum, and Tony had an easy game.

Coach announced that Kevin and Scott would be starting strikers. The starting midfielders included Wayne and Brendan, and Joe would be one of the starting defensemen. Luis felt a sense of security knowing his bandmate would be with him on defense.

That was, if Coach named Luis the starting goalie.

"And finally," Coach Anderson began, "the starting goaltender for this year's River Valley JV Eagles will be—"

Luis held his breath. Papá would be overjoyed if Luis were named starting goalie, but if that happened, so much pressure would be riding on his shoulders. Luis just wasn't sure if that was what he wanted.

"—Tony Smith!"

Coach's words hit Luis like a soccer ball to the stomach. A small cheer went up for Tony.

"You were a solid goalie for us last year, Tony," Coach said, "and I know you'll be even better this year. That's all for today, boys. Be sure to arrive an hour early for warm-ups before Saturday's big game. Rest up tonight and see you then!"

The players headed to the parking lot. Joe put his arm around Luis's shoulder. "It's okay, Lucky. Tony is a year older, and Coach is just getting him ready for varsity. Anyway, I still think you're a better goalie."

"Thanks, Joe."

Kevin caught up with them. "Don't sweat it, Lucky," he said. "You're our secret weapon. Coach will know exactly when to put you in."

Luis nodded and tried to keep his head up. He tried to find his zone. He knew he would eventually, but for now, as he biked home from the field, he just felt sad.

* * *

That Saturday, Luis watched from the bench as the JV Eagles ran circles around the Forestville Bears. It was a beautiful afternoon for the Eagles' home opener. The bleachers were filled with parents and classmates wearing the Eagles' colors of maroon and white. Scott and Kevin had each scored a goal in the first half. The Eagles were winning 2–0.

Papá had taken it hard when Luis said that Coach Anderson hadn't chosen him to be the starting goalie. "We should've spent more time working on your angles," Papá had said, "showing you how to take the net away from the shooter—"

Abuela had interrupted Papá. "He tried his best. There's nothing Luis can do now except watch and learn."

Luis remembered Abuela's words as Coach gave the team a pep talk before the start of the second half. "Joe, keep up the strong defense. Wayne, Brendan, continue pushing the ball up to the strikers. Kevin, Scott, keep blasting shots, and we'll have this wrapped up in no time."

The whistle blew, and the second half began. Watching from the sidelines definitely didn't feel right to Luis. Aside from the scent of mowed grass and the sounds of bugs buzzing around his head, he might as well have been watching the game on TV.

At least then I could play my guitar, Luis thought.

A pair of Bears strikers rushed toward the Eagles' goal. One striker burst past Joe to the front of the net. Tony rushed out to tackle the ball away. The Bears striker passed to his wingman, who slammed the ball into the goal. The visiting crowd cheered. The score was 2–1.

So much for a shutout season, Luis thought. He turned toward the bleachers. Papá pointed at Luis, then stuck out his hands like a goalie making a save. He mouthed the words, *You would've stopped that.*

Luis shrugged. *Maybe,* he thought.

He turned back to the game. The Eagles midfielders kicked the ball back and forth, waiting for Kevin or Scott to get open. Finally, Wayne launched a pass that landed in front of Kevin. He trapped the ball, dribbled past a Bears defender, then sent a high pass to Scott, who headed the ball into the net.

Goal!

The home crowd erupted. Kevin and Scott high-fived and hugged the rest of the team. The game continued on like this until the final whistle. Every player contributed to the Eagles' 6–1 victory.

Every player, it seemed, except Luis.

CHAPTER 8

THE AUDITION

Wednesday crawled by. Luis was so nervous for the talent show audition that he could hardly eat lunch.

"We'll be fine, Lucky," Joe said. Luis, Joe, and Sheena sat together in the cafeteria. "Ms. Mellor is going to love us!"

"Plus we've been rehearsing a lot," Sheena said. "We all know our parts. We're going to be great!"

Still, Luis couldn't help worrying. He still hadn't told his family about the audition. In fact, they didn't even know about Lucky Save. Even if the band did get accepted into the talent show, Papá might not let Luis perform because he'd been keeping secrets.

"Don't sweat it, Lucky," Joe said. "Everything's going to be cool."

The bell rang. The trio slipped into the wave of students leaving the cafeteria. The rest of the day felt just like that: a long, slow wave pushing Luis toward the audition.

* * *

"Okay, Lucky Save," Ms. Mellor said that afternoon. "Let's hear it!"

Luis stepped up to the mic. When they rehearsed in Joe's garage, Luis just shouted over the music. But now, the microphone sent his voice booming through a pair of big, black speakers.

"Hello," he said. The speakers squealed back. Ms. Mellor turned a knob and the noise went away.

"We're Lucky Save. I'm Luis, that's Sheena on bass, and Joe on drums. Our first song is called 'Breakaway.'"

Joe clicked his drumsticks—"One, two, three, four!"—and they kicked into the song.

The low rumble of Sheena's bass filled the room. Joe's drums felt like they were pounding right inside Luis's chest. His entire body vibrated with the music's energy. He started jumping up and down. He couldn't help himself—it was his body's natural response. Luis hardly noticed his hands shaping chords and strumming. It was incredible to hear his own voice booming out of the speakers and blending with the sounds of his guitar, Sheena's bass, and Joe's drums. Luis felt like he was dreaming.

Ms. Mellor clapped and sang along. When they reached the song's end, Joe sent up thunderous explosions of sound. Luis and Sheena jumped high and slammed the final chord with Joe's cymbal crash.

Ms. Mellor gave them a standing ovation. "Bravo!" she said. "That was wonderful!"

"Really?" Luis said, wiping a bit of sweat from his forehead.

"Yes!" Ms. Mellor replied. "You clearly love playing music together. Joe, those drum lessons are really paying off! Sheena, you're a really well-rounded bassist! And Luis, who taught you to sing and play like that?"

Luis shrugged. "It's just how I play."

"Well, you are a natural," Ms. Mellor said. "People are going to love Lucky Save. Do you have more songs?"

"You ever heard of Silver Summer?" Joe shouted.

Ms. Mellor smirked. "Guys, I saw Silver Summer when I was your age."

"You saw Silver Summer?" Luis exclaimed. "In concert?"

Ms. Mellor nodded. "They're one of my favorites."

"Awesome!" Joe said. "We play four of their songs. Luis, let's do 'Catch Me'!"

Luis strummed the opening chords, and then Joe and Sheena joined in. Luis closed his eyes and sang into the mic. He felt a new jolt of energy.

Ms. Mellor sang along the whole time. When they finished, she gave them another standing ovation. "Lucky Save is officially in the talent show," she said. "Since you rock so hard, we'll have you close out the night. How does that sound?"

"Perfect!" Joe and Sheena shouted. Luis was excited, too, but his excitement was mixed with anxiety. Now, he had to tell Papá about Lucky Save. And he'd have to tell him soon.

CHAPTER 9

CLOSE YOUR EYES AND SING

Abuela was so excited when Luis told her about Lucky Save and the band's audition.

"I'm so happy for you." She kissed him on each cheek. "Someday you'll be a famous musician. Your name will be in big lights all around the world!"

Luis tried to imagine it. He had never been anywhere near a stage in his life. But soon he'd be playing to his entire school. He was taking his first steps into a strange and exciting new world.

"What was it like when you were a musician, Abuela?" he asked.

Abuela laughed. "I still am a musician, Luisito. You would have to steal my voice and hands for me to stop."

Luis blushed. "Well, I mean, what was it like playing music when you were, you know, um . . ."

Abuela smiled. "When I was young?"

Luis nodded. Abuela took off her glasses as if that would help her see more clearly into the past. "Well," she started, "it was a much different time. We didn't have the internet and music videos. We had records and the radio. I listened to WMRL out of San Juan. When they played rock and roll, my heart went boom, boom just like a drum. I knew I wanted to make that kind of music."

Luis knew what Abuela meant about music making your heart go boom.

Abuela continued, moving her fingers like she was playing a piano. "I would sit at the piano and pick out those songs with my right hand, making up the chords with my left. I still don't know if they were exactly right, but it felt like magic. My papá didn't like me playing that stuff. He wanted me to play classical music. And I loved that too. But I loved rock and roll more."

"You sang in a band too?" Luis asked.

"Sí. I moved to New York City when I was twenty and started singing in bands. I loved singing. I loved the stage. All those lights, those people, and the music swirling around. It was like being in a completely different world."

Luis smiled. It was amazing to think that there was a time when Abuela was the lead singer in a band.

"Mira, Luisito." Abuela pulled a photograph from her dress pocket. It was square, with torn edges. The color had yellowed with age. Luis wished he could zoom into it like on his cell phone. There was so much happening in the picture. A crowd of people watched a band perform on a stage. There was a bassist, drummer, piano player, and guitarist, all wearing matching black suits.

"His guitar looks like mine!" Luis said.

Abuela nodded.

Center stage, a small woman with long, curly black hair wore a sparkly dress and sang into a microphone.

"Is that . . . ?" Luis asked. He looked up at Abuela.

"Sí," she said. "That's me."

"Wow." Luis held the photo close to his eyes, wishing he could slip through it and into that club to watch Abuela sing. The bass drum said The Misty Trio in big, bubbly letters. "That was the name of your band?"

Abuela nodded while Luis kept staring at the photograph. He studied the musicians' gear and imagined the sound of their music. He had so many questions.

"What song were you playing here?" he started. "Who were the guys in the band? How often did you practice? Who's the most famous person you met? How did you—"

Abuela laughed and put up her hands. "It was so long ago. No me recuerdo! I was very young."

"But, Abuela—"

She smiled. "That'll be you someday, Luisito. Someday very soon! You'll be up on a stage with your band. Then you'll have your own stories to tell."

"How do I do it?" Luis asked, nerves slowly bubbling up in his stomach. "How do I perform for all those people?"

Abuela thought for a minute. "You just close your eyes and sing. That's all I ever did. Just close your eyes and sing."

"I'm scared to tell Papá," Luis said suddenly. "I'm worried that he just wants me to play soccer, and that he'll make me quit music."

Abuela hugged Luis. "Your father just wants you to love the things that he loves. I might have pushed him too hard to play music when he was younger.

Maybe that's why he didn't love it as much. But he loves you, Luisito. He'll support whatever you love to do."

Luis nodded. He felt sad. "Abuela?"

"Yes, Luisito?"

"Do you miss it?"

"Miss what?"

Luis pointed to the photograph.

Abuela smiled, but her eyes looked a little teary. "I'm excited to watch you become a musician." She pointed to the photo. "That's yours now. Keep it. For good luck."

"Muchas gracias, Abuela." Luis slipped the photo into his guitar case and secured the latches for safekeeping.

CHAPTER 10

BREAKAWAY

Halfway into the season, the Eagles were still undefeated. But now, for the first time, the Eagles were losing 2–1 to the Springfield Wildcats.

Kevin had scored first for the Eagles, but then the Wildcats scored twice in a row. Their second goal came off a corner kick. Corner kicks were a goalie's second-worst nightmare, right behind penalty shots. Luis would rather face a thousand corner kicks than one penalty shot.

But the Eagles gathered steam toward the end of the first half. Brendan booted the ball to Kevin, who trapped it near the Wildcats' goal. Scott waved for a pass, but a Wildcats defender blocked him.

"Shoot, Kevin!" Coach Anderson shouted.

Kevin blasted a shot high over the goalie's right shoulder. *Score!* The crowd cheered. The Eagles had tied the score with a minute remaining in the first half.

But the Wildcats attacked hard off the next kickoff. A Wildcats midfielder sent a pass through the air to the Wildcats player wearing number 19. He trapped the ball and dribbled toward the goal. Joe challenged him, and Number 19 passed to his wingman. His feet swished like scissor blades over the ball, confusing Tony, and Number 19 blasted the ball into the net. Cheers erupted from the Wildcats and their fans. The score was 3–2.

A whistle blew for halftime. The players hustled to their benches.

Coach Anderson wasn't pleased. "Our heads are not in this game, Eagles. Let's change our strategy." He looked over at Tony. "I'm going to sit you out for the second half."

Tony nodded and slumped onto the bench.

Coach Anderson looked at Luis. "Luis, you're up. Time to show them why we call you Lucky."

Luis's heart thudded in his chest. His stomach filled with butterflies. His throat went dry. He just nodded and then jogged away from the bench to do his warm-ups.

Nobody could score on you last year, Luis told himself. *That's why they call you Lucky.*

Joe and Kevin approached him. "You're going to be great, Lucky," Joe said. "Just remember your Goalie Zone. Once you're there, nobody can beat you."

Kevin nodded. "Let's win this."

"Thanks, guys," Luis said. "I'll do my best."

The ref blew the whistle to start the second half. For the first time that season, Luis stood in front of the goal. He ran through his ritual and felt focused. He searched the bleachers and saw Papá and Abuela waving at him. Luis waved back, then turned to the game. It was up to him to help his team win.

The Eagles controlled the ball from the start of the second half. Brendan passed to Scott. Scott dribbled past a Wildcat, then sailed a pass to Kevin. He deked around a Wildcats defender, and suddenly he was all alone in front of the Wildcats' goal. He faked out the goalie, then slammed the ball into the right corner.

Score!

The crowd cheered. Kevin had tied the game!

Following the next kickoff, the Wildcats midfielders passed the ball back and forth, waiting for their strikers to get into position. Finally, one midfielder connected a pass with Number 19, who dribbled toward the goal.

Luis took a deep breath, watching the striker closely. Number 19 was their best player. Luis had to stop him.

Joe tried to strip the ball away, but it bounced off the striker's shin guards and rolled toward another Wildcat.

Luis sprang into action. He rushed forward just as Number 19 was gearing up to kick. The shot smashed Luis in the stomach like a cannonball. But he collapsed onto the ball, preventing a rebound.

A cheer went up in the crowd. Luis had made his first save! He waited for his teammates to get into position, then kicked the ball to midfield.

It landed right by Brendan, who dribbled onto the Wildcats' side and fired a pass to Scott. He worked around a Wildcats defender and blasted a shot on net. The Wildcats goalie made the save but spilled the rebound. Wildcats defenders scrambled to clear the ball. Kevin rushed in quick as lightning and booted the ball into the goal. The score was 4–3. The Eagles were now winning!

After Kevin scored his third goal, the Wildcats kept a tight defense on the Eagles player. For a while, the game turned into passing drills at centerfield. But the longer the ball stayed away from Luis, the calmer he felt.

Time ticked away. Soon Coach Anderson cupped his hand around his mouth and yelled to his players, "Two minutes left, Eagles! Keep it up!"

Excitement flooded Luis. He was two minutes away from his first win as a JV goalie! The crowd started cheering and whistling. Luis scanned the crowd for Papá and Abuela and saw them cheering.

Then two Wildcats strikers broke through midfield and rushed toward the goal. One of them was Number 19. Luis's heart began racing. The crowd cheered louder. Luis watched for the striker's tell, trying to judge if he would pass or shoot. When Joe blocked the other Wildcats striker, Luis figured Number 19 would soon take a shot. Luis knew Number 19 liked to aim for the top-left corner. He felt a magnetic pull toward that side of the net.

Number 19 was about to shoot when Joe stuck out his leg and tripped him. The striker went tumbling to the ground. The referee blew a whistle, threw up a yellow card, and shouted the words Luis feared most: *"Penalty kick!"*

Coach Anderson shouted from the sidelines, "It's been two minutes! The game is over!"

The ref shook his head and tapped his watch. "Two seconds left."

Luis let out a deep breath. This was it. The game had landed on his shoulders. If Number 19 scored, they'd go into overtime. If Luis made the save, the Eagles would win.

Then, from somewhere deep in the crowd, Luis heard a voice chanting, *"Lucky, Lucky, Lucky!"* It was Papá! More voices joined in, and soon the entire Eagles crowd was chanting Luis's nickname.

Luis closed his eyes and pictured Papá dribbling around Abuela's backyard. He heard music floating through the air and thought of Abuela. He heard The Strikers singing "Breakaway." He nervously started singing under his breath.

Luis went deep into his Goalie Zone and fell into the rhythm of the song. The referee blew the whistle. Luis opened his eyes. He was ready.

Number 19 looked up from the ball and gazed quickly at the goal's top-left corner, then back at Luis. It was no more than a blink of an eye. But Luis saw it. That was where the ball would go. Luis steadied himself, preparing to leap in that direction.

It happened in a flash. Number 19 fired the ball high, hard, and exactly where Luis imagined. Luis shot off like a rocket. The ball was just out of reach for Luis to catch, but his outstretched fingers were enough to stop the ball. It spiraled through the air, and as Luis fell to the ground, he opened his arms and caught it at the edge of the goalpost.

The ref blew the whistle. "Game over!" he shouted.

The crowd roared. Luis's teammates surrounded him, high-fiving and clapping him on the back. On the bench, Coach Anderson cheered. In the stands, Papá and Abuela hugged and pumped their fists in the air. The cheering turned into a chorus of "Breakaway" in Luis's mind. He had done it. Luis had saved the game.

* * *

The next day, Coach Anderson called Luis to his office after school. "The varsity Eagles backup goalie got injured during a game last week. They need a replacement. Coach Bergan saw your penalty kick save. He wants you to join the varsity squad as a backup."

Luis's heart started pounding. He and Joe had gone to a few varsity games throughout the season. Those players were huge.

"When is the game?" Luis asked.

"Next Saturday night in Ellicottville."

Luis felt like a soccer ball had smacked him in the gut. *That's the same night as the talent show!*

"It would be a great learning experience," Coach continued. "Even just watching from the bench will make you a stronger player."

"What about Tony?" Luis asked.

Coach Anderson shrugged. "Coach Bergan asked about you."

Luis sat silently for a moment. This was a big deal. Papá would be really proud of him. He would want Luis to say yes. But then Luis would be with the varsity team in Ellicottville on the night of the talent show. He didn't want to let Lucky Save down. On top of it all, he still hadn't told Papá about the band or the talent show.

Finally, Luis said, "I have to talk to my dad."

Coach Anderson nodded. Luis left and sighed to himself. He knew what he'd said was true. It was time.

CHAPTER 11

LUCKY SAVE

Papá was thrilled when Luis told him the news after dinner that night. "The coaches see you as the future," Papá said. "Winning teams are built on strong goalies!"

"I know, Papá," Luis replied. "But . . ."

Papá frowned. "But *what*? This is amazing news!"

"Well . . ." Luis took a deep breath and began telling Papá all about the band. He told him how he had been playing music, not soccer, at Joe's house. He told Papá about the talent show and how Ms. Mellor wanted them to finish out the whole event. He even told him that although Joe had green hair, he was a good student and a great friend.

"The talent show is the same night as the varsity game," Luis finished. "If I join varsity, I won't be able to perform. I've been really nervous that you'll be mad and won't let me play in the talent show anyway."

Papá took a deep breath. "Mad at you? Luis, a few weeks ago, I saw you biking with your guitar on your back. I figured you were playing music with somebody," Papá said, smiling. "What's your band called?"

"Lucky Save."

"That's a great name," he said. "Do you play songs about soccer?"

Luis nodded. "We play 'Breakaway'!"

Papá smiled. "My favorite!" He glanced at Luis's open guitar case, and there he noticed the old photo of Abuela. Papá picked it up. "What's this?"

"Abuela gave it to me," Luis said. "That's her."

"Where?" Papá asked.

"The singer."

Papá held the photo closer to his eyes. "Oh, my goodness." He stared hard at the photo for a moment. Then he said, "Music skipped me, but you've got it, hijo. That's Abuela's gift to you. And, well, you have to use it."

Luis didn't know what to say. For the first time, he felt like Papá understood. It wasn't really a choice. Music had chosen him.

"I still think you should consider the offer to play for varsity, though," Papá said, setting down the photo. "Music might keep you mentally strong, but soccer keeps you physically strong. That balance is important."

Luis smiled. "I'm not quitting soccer, Papá," he said. "But there has to be room for both."

"I'll talk to Coach Anderson and Coach Bergan." Papá handed Luis his guitar. "Play me a song?"

Backstage at the River Valley Auditorium, Luis felt familiar butterflies in his stomach. Except instead of winning a soccer game, he'd have to win over an audience. He peeked out from behind the curtain. The auditorium was packed. The audience was watching a dance troupe spin around the stage in sparkly outfits.

Coach Anderson sat with the soccer team. Luis had admitted that he didn't want to join varsity just yet, and Coach understood. Tony would fill in for the injured varsity goalie. And Luis would be the JV starting goalie for the rest of the season. That was even better!

Papá and Abuela sat in the front row. Abuela wore a glittery red dress and a gold necklace. Papá had dressed up in a suit but wore his soccer shoes for luck.

Joe and Sheena came up behind Luis. "Ready to rock, Lucky?" Joe asked. He twirled a drumstick between his fingers.

"Lots of people out there," Luis said.

"It's a sellout crowd!" Sheena said. "They cheered really loud for the jazz band."

"It's just like a soccer game," Joe said. "The home crowd is here to cheer us on!"

Joe had spiked his green hair into a mohawk. Luis had slicked his hair back. They were both wearing black suits with white shirts and skinny black ties, just like The Strikers. Sheena wore dark eyeliner, silver glitter on her cheeks, a black dress, and black boots.

Ms. Mellor approached them. "You three look great! Just like a real rock band!"

"Thanks, Ms. M!" Joe said.

"The show choir is up next, and then you guys are on," Ms. Mellor said.

The butterflies in Luis's stomach flapped up into his throat. He'd never felt more anxious in his life.

"Are you nervous, Luis?" Ms. Mellor asked.

"A little," he croaked.

"It's okay to feel nervous," Ms. Mellor replied. "It's extra energy your body makes for your performance. Once you start playing, you'll relax. Just like you did in your audition. You'll be great."

Luis went to his guitar case and pulled out the old photo of Abuela. His hands shook as he brought it close to his eyes. He hoped to channel her musical energy.

Joe and Sheena came over as Luis tucked the photo away in his case. "Listen, Lucky," Joe said. "We're both nervous too. But I know it's all going to go away as soon as we hit the first note. Our music turns off all that stuff."

Luis nodded. Hearing that Joe and Sheena were also nervous made Luis feel less scared.

Luis smiled. "I love playing music with you two. I can't wait to start practicing for our next gig!" Saying that to Joe and Sheena made his heart swell, and suddenly Luis felt like he could take flight. The trio hugged. They were ready.

Luis closed his eyes and remembered his penalty kick save. He remembered breathing deeply and trusting that his body would know what to do. He remembered Papá and Abuela rooting for him. They were here tonight too. Even though he would be on a huge stage in front of hundreds of people, he could pretend he was just playing for them.

Cheers rose from the audience as the show choir finished performing. Ms. Mellor rushed up to the trio before going onstage to introduce them. "You're on!"

Luis gave her a thumbs-up. Ms. Mellor hurried onstage, and soon her voice echoed through the auditorium. "Thank you, everyone! For tonight's final performance, we have a very special act. I'm sure they'll have you jumping out of your seats! Give it up for River Valley Junior High's very own rock band, Lucky Save!"

The crowd cheered as Luis, Joe, and Sheena stepped onto the stage. White lights blinded Luis.

He plugged his guitar into his amp. Sheena slung her bass over her shoulder. Joe rolled the snare drum and crashed his cymbals. The crowd cheered.

Luis stepped up to the microphone. "Hello, River Valley." His voice boomed through the sound system. "We are Lucky Save. This first song is called 'Breakaway.'"

The soccer team cheered. In the front row, Papá held up his cell phone to film.

Abuela blew him kisses.

Behind him, Joe clicked his drumsticks.

"One, two, three, four!"

Luis took a deep breath, closed his eyes, and sang.

GLOSSARY

amp (AMP)—short for *amplifier*; a machine used to make instruments sound louder

anxiety (ang-ZYE-uh-tee)—a feeling of worry or fear; to feel anxious is to experience anxiety

deke (DEEK)—to fake an opponent out of position

dribble (DRIB-uhl)—to move the ball along by kicking it with your feet

harmony (HAR-muh-nee)—a set of musical notes played at the same time; the notes blend together to form harmony

reflex (REE-fleks)—an action that happens without a person's control or effort

ritual (RICH-oo-uhl)—a set of actions that is always done in the same way

scrimmage (SKRIM-ij)—a practice game

strategy (STRAT-uh-jee)—a careful plan or method

striker (STRAHY-ker)—a player whose main responsibility is to score; also called a forward

vintage (VIN-tij)—from the past

SPANISH GLOSSARY

abuela—grandmother

arroz con gandules—rice with pigeon peas; a traditional Puerto Rican dish often served at holidays

Dios mío—oh my God

gracias—thank you; *muchas gracias* means thank you very much

hijo—son

hola—hello

mi—my

mira—look

nieto—grandchild

no me recuerdo—I don't remember

por favor—please

que pasó—what happened

sí—yes

un poquito—a little

vamos—let's go

DISCUSSION QUESTIONS

1. Luis is often nervous before soccer games and band performances. What are some things that he does to calm himself? What do you do when you feel nervous?

2. Luis likes playing soccer, but he *loves* playing music. Are there some things that you like to do and others that you love to do?

3. At the beginning of the story, Luis is the "new kid" in River Valley. Have you ever been new to a school, team, or other group? How did it feel? What did others do to make you comfortable?

WRITING PROMPTS

1. Write a list of similarities and differences between being on a soccer team and being in a band. Then, pick one of each and write a paragraph explaining it.

2. When Abuela was young, she was a singer in New York City. Write a letter that you imagine she wrote home to her parents during this time.

3. In Chapter 10, Luis makes an important save for his team. Imagine Luis misses the penalty kick instead. What might have happened next? How would Luis have felt? Rewrite the end of the chapter.

FUN FACTS
ABOUT SOCCER

When a soccer player scores three goals in a single game, it is called a hat trick. A "perfect hat trick" can be achieved by scoring one goal with the right foot, one goal with the left foot, and one goal with the head.

A professional regulation soccer goal is 8 feet (2.44 meters) tall and 24 feet (7.32 m) wide. Youth soccer goals are slightly smaller, making them easier to tend for younger players.

Goaltending is both physically and mentally demanding. Goalies often practice meditation to help them stay calm during games.

Soccer is the world's most popular sport, with an estimated 3.5 billion fans and 265 million players.

In British English, soccer is known as football. The Spanish translation is *fútbol*.

The earliest soccer balls were pig bladders wrapped in leather! It wasn't until 1855 that Charles Goodyear made the first soccer ball out of rubber. In the 1960s, the iconic black-and-white hexagon pattern known on modern soccer balls was created.

The biggest soccer tournament in the world is the FIFA (Fédération Internationale de Football Association) World Cup. It's held every four years and may be the most popular sporting event in the world.

LOOKING FOR MORE SIZZLING
SOCCER ACTION?
THEN PICK UP ...

JAKE MADDOX JV

SOCCER
STAND-OFF

ABOUT the AUTHOR

Colin Scharf has been a writer and musician for twenty years. He lives in Mankato, Minnesota, with his wife, Laura (who is also a singer/songwriter), and their cat, Marty. Colin and Laura have a band called Good Night Gold Dust. Their music can be found at www.goodnightgolddust.com